PUPPY ROUNDUP!

By Margo Lundell 🐾 Illustrated by Josie Yee

 A GOLDEN BOOK • NEW YORK

Golden Books Publishing Company, Inc., Racine, Wisconsin 53404

© 1996 Disney Enterprises, Inc. Based on the book by Dodie Smith, published by Viking Press, Inc. All rights reserved. Printed in the U.S.A. No part of this book may be reproduced or copied in any form without written permission from the copyright owner. GOLDEN BOOKS & DESIGN™, A GOLDEN BOOK®, A FIRST LITTLE GOLDEN BOOK®, and the distinctive gold spine are trademarks of Golden Books Publishing Company, Inc. Library of Congress Catalog Card Number: 95-79811 ISBN: 0-307-98754-X   MCMXCVI

In the beginning, when their family was small,
Pongo and Perdita had fifteen adorable puppies—
who poked their noses into everything!

They loved playing hide-and-seek.
The puppy named Patch liked to hide
in the laundry basket.

One day Roger and Anita decided to have a family portrait taken at the photographer's studio.

"Round up the puppies," Roger told Pongo and Perdita. Then he wondered, "Now, where are my car keys?"

Pongo and Perdita went to hunt for the puppies and the car keys, too. In the parlor they found three playful puppies—but no keys.

"Hurry, puppies," said Pongo.
"Follow me to the kitchen."

Perdita went upstairs to look for the other puppies.

In the bedroom Perdita spied seven
frisky puppies—but no keys.

"Come along," Perdita told the puppies.
"We're going to have our picture taken."

Meanwhile Pongo trotted up to the music room.
Could the rest of the puppies be there?

What luck! Pongo found four more puppies in the music room—but still no keys.

Pongo led the puppies to the kitchen. Then there was just one puppy left to find: Patch. And Perdita thought she knew where he might be. Was she right?

Yes! Perdita found Patch in the bathroom,
hiding in the laundry basket.

Patch scampered after his mother. Perdita
didn't know it, but the puppy was dragging
a pair of Roger's pants with him!

"The last puppy!" Roger shouted when he saw Patch. As Roger pulled the pants away from the little dog, he heard a jingling sound.

"Look what Patch found!" Roger cried. "My keys!"
"Hooray!" Anita said. "Now let's go to the studio."

Fifteen adorable puppies posed for their
photograph with their proud parents. A perfect
picture—at last!